TABOO SEX STORIES
EXPLICIT DIRTY EROTICA SHORT STORIES

CHARA GLADEY

plicit Press

CHAPTER 1

FORGIVE ME, FATHER

THE DARKNESS of the booth is the perfect setting for her confession. Tandy is twenty but her conscience is still intact, sort of. The conservative knee-length skirt and pastel blouse make for the perfect wardrobe, even if Father Fisher won't be able to see her. She just needs to get her indiscretion out in the open and off her chest. The woody smell of the booth is almost overwhelming. It's obviously just been polished. Just before the smell becomes the sole focus of her attention, the wooden-square slides open and she receives a solemn greeting from father Fisher.

She jumps straight into her confession:

"Forgive me father for I have sinned. It's been four weeks since my last confession. In this time I have had sexual intercourse with a man who is not my husband." Her tone is low and husky like you would expect a call girl on a sex hotline to sound. It is this tone that has Father Fisher in a trance almost instantly so that he doesn't interrupt her. A part of him *wants* her to continue. She does...

"He wasn't the type of man I would normally even look at, but something about him drew me in. Perhaps it was the

way he seemed to control the entire world every time he gave us an order.

Whatever it was, I wanted him from the second he opened his mouth. So when we were finally alone in the office, I couldn't help myself, I just needed to get close to him. And so I did.

I could smell him under his shirt. It was a mix of sweat, cigarettes, and expensive cologne. Twice my age, maybe more, but I wanted nothing more than to be close to him. The thought consumed me almost as completely as the fire burning between my legs. The hotter it became, the closer I moved to him. He made no attempts to move away and before I knew exactly what it was that I was going to do when I got to him, I was there. He just gave me a knowing look, then an approving nod. I took that to mean that he too wanted me. But he did nothing. He just stood there and looked at me as if whatever I decided to do would be okay.

My fingers found the bulge in his pants. His breathing immediately quickened, deepened. I gave the dome a firm squeeze and the cock underneath his chinos immediately stiffened. This confirmed his attraction to me and my own desire for him was sealed. I got to my knees and worked on his buckle until his pants came undone, dropping to the floor. He still wore underpants, something that amused me. I hid my smile.

Over the red of his briefs, I bit gently into his manhood. The size of it was as impressive as its strength, the solidity of his erection hinting at its potential power. I kept biting up and down the entire length of his massive cock, the tool hardening more and more with each nibble. I wanted to taste the flesh under the fabric so I pulled on the briefs, the elastic giving easily so that the underwear joined his chinos at his knees. He leaned back onto the desk and held on to its edge. I came up to where his balls hung low and took the massive sack in my mouth.

The smell of cologne and cigarettes still lingered, hanging heavier in the air now that the room seemed to heat up. I started sweating down my breasts too and so I touched myself, my mouth still snugging around the balls. He let out little whimpers as I bit into his sack and then sucked.

Biting and sucking, licking him, he started to stagger from foot to foot, his cock straight and solid above my head. I let go of myself and reached for his tool, pulling it down gently as I continued my oral fixation on his sack. His guttural moans excited me and so I kept at it.

On my knees, and with his cock in hand and pointed in the direction of my mouth, he eased himself a little lower. This allowed me to comfortably ease him into my mouth without straining my neck. I showed my appreciation by taking all of him into me, something that excited him as much as it did me. I knew from the second I took him into my mouth that I would enjoy it just as much as he did, if not more. So I dragged it out as long as I could. Catching his eyes I knew that he was happy that I did because he closed them, and for the longest time they remained shut.

His cock tasted every bit as good as it smelled. I sucked on every part of it, savoring certain bits, lingering particularly on the head. Every time I got to the base, the entire thing in my mouth, he would open his eyes briefly to take in my achievement. I wanted to please him. I needed to please him. I gave him the longest, most sensual blow job I could manage, and when his cock started to leak into my mouth I knew that I was definitely handling him well. A few more deep-throat movements and the stream coming from the tip of his cock into my mouth was a steady flow. I knew that I could milk him for more though.

With much effort, I managed to get myself off his cock and to my feet. It was hard to remove his cock from my mouth because it just tasted so good. On my feet, I took in his scent in deep breaths at his neck. He held me to him and breathed in my hair. I took his cock in my hands and moved it to my pussy, which ached for him now. There was no time to think of anything else. I just wanted him to get inside me. He just held my head to his neck, not really involving himself. I sensed that he was simply allowing me to use his cock. The ring on his finger probably had a lot to do with it. But I just needed what I needed so I ignored the band. It was clear to me though that it was a battle of biology and psychology for him, and fortunately for me, his biology was winning.

It would have been easier for me to remove my panties but my lust had consumed me by then. I pulled them to the side with one hand and his cock in the other while he dressed my head in kisses. I accepted that he wouldn't kiss me on my mouth so I focused on his cock, which is what I wanted anyway. The whimpers from his mouth let me know that the heat inside my cunt weaved enough of a spell on him. I needed only to make the introduction, a few inches before he took over the job of penetrating me. He pushed himself up into me fast and hard, and immediately he began to thrust. Each stroke was a fire.

The power in his cock surprised me, even though I could feel that it was possible that it would be formidable. Its presence inside me took me to places I can't remember ever being in my entire life. Every time he seemed to take hours to withdraw, and only seconds to fully reclaim my cunt. His cock moved so slowly out of me that his rapid reinsertion jolted me back from cloud nine. He fucked me with the experience of somebody who has robust sex several times a day every day. I allowed myself for a minute to wish I was the woman underneath him every day, every night. I let myself wonder what it might be like to have mine be the pussy he plundered on demand; But only for a minute...

Before I could register the absence of his cock it was removed. He pushed me hard against the desk and then down on it. I felt the spit on my ass just before he started rubbing it into my hole. I knew he wouldn't want to cum inside my pussy and so I accepted that this was his alternative. I would have rather he came in my mouth but there was no time to speak before he rammed his cock into me, my ass stretched wide fast. I tried hard not to scream, succeeding. His immediate ramming, his pounding softened me up quickly, and soon received him easily. He started to fuck me hard almost as soon as the elastic of my tiny ring gave way. His cock in my ass was a thousand times more commanding than it had been in my cunt. I loved it, the way he took me the way he wanted and didn't give a fuck.

He started to fill my hole with fiery hot cum before his fingers dug into my cunt. Despite the stream shooting into me he continued to thrust hard and fast. His pounding persisted from the time it took him to get four fingers into my vagina, pull it wide apart, and then milk it completely. My pussy sprayed such a massive load it looked like my water had broken. Still, his thrusting into my ass continued. It was a minute before I realized that he was still fucking me, getting himself to a second orgasm. He came again before eventually slowing down. After he pulled his cock from me a turned to face him, and couldn't resist taking his balls into my mouth again. He pulled on his cock above my head while I sucked his balls. His third load rained down on me minutes later. He took my cunt into his mouth and brought me to two further orgasms before we sorted out the space and I left him to his wedding ring and his conscience...

So, father, you understand that I've been very, very bad..." Suddenly Tandy is silent, unable to speak anymore. Peering into her part of the cubicle Father Fisher sees that her panties are at her knees and her fingers have disappeared up her skirt. He sits back down and listens to her bring herself to a massive orgasm. She kicks into the wood and bangs on it as her fingers draw the most incredible pressure from her cunt. He slams the tiny door shut and lets his own hand fall onto his cock, although not directly. Over the layers of fabric, his cock is a solid length of hardness, the sensation not as intense as he could have made it if he had just lifted his garment and touched his prick. But this is all he needs to bring himself to a mild orgasm leaving him with a sense that maybe he too should make a confession of his own...

CHAPTER 2

HER SISTER'S DRUTHERS

LENA HEARD Ryan's car roll into the driveway. She heard his footsteps in the hallway, and then he appeared in the living room. He stopped midway when he saw Lena standing naked in the middle of the living room.

He cursed, "Hey, get some clothes on, what's the matter with you?"

Lena covered the distance with a few quick steps. She rubbed her body against her brother-in- law's sinewy built. He was so dashing and muscular; she had always wanted to do this.

Lena kissed Ryan full on the lips as her hands dropped down to caress his penis. "C'mon," Lena murmured to his ear. "Your wife is fucking someone else too."

She kissed his neck and nibbled his ears, as his fingers played his manhood with increasing urgency. He was growing erect, unable to prevent his arousal from mounting. Lena had already pulled his pants down and she knelt before him in supplication as she held his red, angry penis in her hand and ran her fingers tenderly up and down his shaft.

Ryan grunted in joy and let go of his defenses as Lena took his penis into her mouth as she sucked and licked him. Lena felt triumph as her brother-in-law surrendered himself to her pleasurable ministrations.

Lena's half-sister Myrna was a mean-spirited woman, who flirted with every attractive man she met. She also inflicted considerable physical and emotional pain on Lena so she decided to take revenge by seducing her husband to be her lover.

It was one of those nasty nights when Myrna slapped her because she had forgotten to send the package Myrna instructed her to mail. After slapping her, Myrna cursed and stormed out of the house, and now Ryan was her slave, ready to prostrate himself before her.

Suddenly, they both heard the roar of Myrna's SUV as it parked in the driveway. "Fuck," Ryan's red face showed his dismay.

His penis was rock-hard and Myrna would surely notice. Ryan pulled Lena to her feet and led her to the back door into the nearby trees.

They ran farther down the cobbled path. They were both half-naked; Lena had managed to grab her dress from the floor, where she dropped it. They could hear Myrna calling for Ryan. Then her voice faded in the distance. They were lucky it was summer and the evening was warm.

Ryan pushed her against a tree and was the aggressor now, as he sought her tongue and twirled and sucked it with her own. He ran his fingers up and down her pussy as his lips left her lips to descend into her hard and tingling nipples.

Lena had her hands on his penis too, firmly massaging

his penis with slow erotic movements. How come Myrna still preferred other men's penis to her husband's? He had an unbelievably firm and sturdy penis that any woman would die for.

She sucked his lower lip as his fingers concentrated on her clit while she played with his dick. Then he groaned and lifted her up to his waiting penis by spreading her thighs and holding each of them with his hands. Lena's arms encircled Ryan's neck as she clung to him.

Then Lena started sliding up and down Ryan's manhood. Lena was producing cooing sounds as the delightful sensations emanated from her pussy and her clit. While she slid down, she pressed her big breasts against his chest and allowed his lips to catch one of her nipples.

Ryan was becoming mad with lust as Lena's moist, hot vagina enclosed his erect penis. In the shadows of the trees, they clung to each other, Ryan going in and out of Lena's pussy and thrusting hard to grind his dick into her juicy opening.

They could hear Myrna calling out to Ryan, but they were unmindful of her shouts because they were both deafened by their lust and frenzied groans to reach their climax.

In a standing position, Ryan rammed his penis into Lena's pussy, grunting in pleasure as his dick got enclosed in a tight embrace by her vagina. They sucked each other's lips and tongues as flesh slapped against flesh and their groins met with wanton abandon.

"You're so hot," Ryan murmured against Lena's lips. "We've got to do this more often."

Lena could hardly speak because the exquisite sensations coming from her groin were nearing its peak. She moved her body up and down Ryan's hot dick and pressed her tits against his chest as she went up and down, pressing on his shoulders with her arms as she went up.

The delightful sensations were driving her wild and ablaze with passion. Suddenly, Myrna's voice echoed in the distance. She had come out of the house and was calling out to Ryan.

But Ryan was beyond caring as he humped Lena, savoring her warm, tight pussy, and sucking her hot, sweet tongue. Faster, he thrust in and out, ramming Lena with his ramrod dick, faster and faster, his face a beet red with his nearing climax.

Lena was moaning, whispering crazily as she arched her back and came in one long, huge orgasm. A few seconds after, Ryan grunted and clasped her tight as his own orgasm came and their love juices mixed, and slowly trickled down to their thighs.

They were startled when Myrna's voice became louder; she was moving towards them. Lena and Ryan seemed to awaken from a trance. They separated almost painfully, their juices still flowing.

"Stay here and hide, I'll go first," Ryan instructed Lena.

Then he ran, half-naked, towards their garage.

Lena hid behind the bushes as Myrna passed close by. She held her pussy and gently caressed it as her orgasm was still slowly ebbing. The lips of her wet vagina were quivering with the aftereffects of a fully satiated desire. She knew she and Ryan would do it again; she was Ryan's first girlfriend anyway. Myrna was just devious and lied to them that Ryan got her pregnant.

CHAPTER 3

MY BROTHER, MY KEEPER (FAMILY TIES)

AT SEVENTEEN BOTH Slevin and Alice are old enough not to care that their parents have decided to marry. They both resolve not to have their lives turned upside down by the fact that today their families merge, moving into the new house where they are supposed to start their new lives as a unit. The two choose their rooms; unpack their stuff and then the family sits down for its first dinner together as one. Alice, a cheerleader, is pleased that at the very least her new brother is hot. He isn't a jock, but the nerdy computer geek knows that even a straight-A student looks better in a six-pack. She can't keep her eyes off of him.

Alice herself is every bit a cheerleader, toned and perfect. Her pretty face is hard to miss while Slevin brushes his teeth, catching her in the mirror and staring at him for the umpteenth time. He tries not to let his eyes betray his teen lust and focuses on cleaning his mouth instead. She disappears from the doorway and goes to her own bathroom to get ready for bed. Both of them try once in their beds to see each other how their parents would like them to see each other, as brother and sister. They try in vain to forget about the perfections of each other's genetic makeup and get some sleep. Sleep doesn't come easy.

By midnight Slevin is unable to pretend that the throbbing erection under his covers has nothing to do with his sister down the hall. He throws the covers off and pulls his cock from under his shorts. He pulls on it for a while but feels that it would be such a waste of a good erection if in fact all the signals he'd been getting from Alice all night meant what his instinct is telling him. Alice isn't a dumb, pretty girl who just happens to have a propensity to cheer. She is intelligent and knows what she wants. This is clear from her achievements and her college options as they were discussed over dinner. So Slevin slithers out of bed, nothing on but boxers over his rock-hard dick, and tiptoes down the hall.

Alice's bedroom door is closed. For a moment Slevin pauses, disappointed. He contemplates the idea of having to masturbate after building himself up so much; it will be unsatisfactory, to say the least. He stands in the dark hall and listens for movement elsewhere in the house. There will be no acceptable explanation that he would possibly be able to give her father as to why he is standing with a huge erection and no t-shirt on outside his seventeen-year-old daughter's bedroom. He wonders if he should knock, or maybe just open the door and have a stupid question to ask his new sister if things turn out to be nothing like he's hoping. But then the door opens, and in nothing but her panties and a cheerleading t-shirt, Alice pulls him in and then instructs him to shut the fuck up by placing a slender finger on his full red lips.

Slevin pulls his shorts off as he follows Alice to the bed. Alice has taken her top off too by the time she gets to the bed. He pushes her onto her back amidst a mature gray silk spread, and she parts and raises her legs for him. Slevin slides her panties off and watches Alice move back on the bed towards the pillows and get comfortable. Her parted legs reveal a perfectly shaven cunt that has thick full lips and a perfect pink pea perched above the entrance to her pussy. Slevin is on the bed moving towards the cunt, on all fours, looking like a menacing lusty tiger. Alice licks her lips, her arousal heavy in her almond eyes.

His mouth is on her pussy first. He takes the clean cunt between his lips and then sends his tongue into it. Alice places her fingers on his head and pushes him onto her vagina while pushing her vagina into his mouth. He eats her pussy out deep, pulling cunt-juice into his mouth, turning himself on immensely. Alice uses her agility to swivel in the direction of Slevin's cock. She does this by wrapping her legs around his neck and then slithering on her back in a half-moon until his dick hangs above her head. Slevin lowers his cock without lifting his head. Alice raises her head to meet the meat and sucks on the rock python hard. It's clear instantly that Alice knows how to suck a dick.

Slevin fucks down deep into Alice's mouth, his suction power pulling liquid from deep inside her pussy at the same time. More and more of her excitement fills his mouth and Slevin realizes that his sister is as turned on as she's going to be. This isn't about long drawn-out lovemaking anyway so she pulls his tongue from inside her and then very slowly eases his dick from her mouth. They face each other now, a question shared between them, and then Alice finds her gym bag. She unwraps the condom herself and then removes her brother's hand from his cock, which he has been stroking in her short absence. She rolls the condom down his solid shaft and then feathers his balls with her fingers for a moment.

Almost as if to torture him just a little more she goes down into a very low sphinx position and sucks on his balls. She licks over the nuts and at the base of the shaft that isn't covered. She bites halfway up the shaft over the condom, sending Slevin's cock into a delirium. Her fingers find her own pussy and she digs into herself. This gives her immense pleasure because her moaning gets progressively louder. Slevin wants to quiet her a bit but his cock has completely taken over his faculties. He watches her hand move about between her legs without actually seeing between her legs because of her position. But just the knowledge of what she is doing keeps his cock engorged.

Then, to torture him further, or please herself a little more, Alice turns onto her back in one movement so that Slevin, upon lifting himself onto his knees, can have his entire sack sink into her mouth. She sucks on the sack, now completely in her mouth. Her fingers move wildly in her vagina now, her knees bent and legs open. Slevin has an awesome view of the cunt he is about to shred with his primed cock but lets Alice do what she's doing for a little bit longer. He manages to hold his cock in check by running his palms over the entire surface of his dick from time to time as Alice gets her cunt to its most absolute receptive. She raises her breasts by arching her back so that her mouth is freed from underneath Slevin and she is again facing him, still on her back though. He watches as she slowly removes the last of her fingers from her cunt and licks them clean. It's showtime.

As he leans over she lifts her legs over his back. She wraps them so tightly that her cunt lifts off the bed in the direction of Slevin's cock. The length of his dick though means that it passes her cunt and hangs somewhere behind her ass. He has to take it in hand and push her off her perch gently. She's back on the bed completely when he is finally able to position his head where it needs to be. He drives his cock into her slowly, enjoying the look on her face as she realizes that he has the kind of cock control that can only come with considerable sexual experience. She realizes that there is probably little that she can do that will impress the hot nerd who's clearly been fucking for longer than she has.

Her legs wrap around him again as he lifts her off the bed. Slevin rests on his heels, his entire weight on his knees. His strong thighs are taught and tight as he lifts Alice completely onto himself now, her legs around his waist. He eases her down onto his dick almost completely, and she rests her elbows on his shoulders to stop him from impaling her completely. Slevin holds her by the waist and moves her up and down on his dick. Leveraging herself on his shoulders, the athletic Alice assumes the reigns herself and starts to ride Slevin's cock with the only help from him being that he is holding them up.

The perfection of the motion lulls them both into a pleasure frenzy. They lose themselves in each other for a long while, unaware of any sounds in the room. They are not even aware of the sounds escaping themselves. When Alice's cunt requires more cock she forces herself down low onto Slevin, who immediately is back in the present. The complete penetration is perceived as a challenge and he pushes himself up and then forward. Without losing any of the space that he has assumed inside her he eases them both onto the bed. He is on top of her and thrusting deep into her in seconds. Again they are both lost in the delirium of forbidden fucking.

There are moments when it seems they might kiss. Both of them avoid being the ones to make this moment happen. This needs to be about nothing but fucking and so kissing is definitely out of the question. The closest they get is biting into each other's ears and necks. Slevin distracts them both from the desire for each other's lips by thrusting harder into her, so hard in fact that her head hits the back of her bed. The soft thumping against the headboard isn't significant enough to cause any alarm. He keeps thrusting harder and harder, trying to get to his end, but also not wanting to do this before Alice is satisfied. She starts to push down against his thrusting herself so he knows that she isn't too far off.

The sound of her alarm is unexpected. Why on earth would anyone set their alarm for four-thirty? Why would Alice get up so early? He looks around for the alarm, which is on the desk near the window, next to her laptop. She would have to get up to turn it off. This is clever if you really want to force yourself from bed. In the center of the room is a yoga mat. This is probably the reason for the early morning. To add to the confirmation that they'd been fucking for hours, the summer sun already started to creep into the room. The house will stir awake very shortly. It's time for Slevin to throw his back into it so that at the very least he can bring Alice to a fucking awesome orgasm. He does just this.

No longer thrusting in long deep strokes he sends his dick into her completely. Then he thrusts in exaggerated circles without pulling a centimeter of his cock from Alice's pussy. This motion brings loud breathing and heavy moaning from her. The alarm is the only thing louder than Alice in the room as Slevin stirs her pussy way past to begin and completely over the edge. She pushes up on his sculpted chest and digs her fingers into his flesh as he makes several final digs into her to finalize her orgasms. He lets her pull him down to herself and returns her tight embrace. She whispers in his ear that she knows he still needs to cum.

They both look at the alarm buzzing itself towards the edge of the table.

Slevin closes his eyes as the sun turns the room orange. He resumes his long thrusts and sends his cock into the depths of her cunt repeatedly. Over and over he is inside her cunt completely, Alice squeezing every muscle in her pussy so tight that her ejaculation does nothing to diminish the friction in her vagina. Slevin sends himself to the other side just as the alarm clock hits the floor and his climax is a mixture of heavy grunts and giggles. They look at the clock on the floor, still buzzing, and hang ten for Slevin to stir around in her pussy for a minute longer, until his cock starts to go limp. He pulls his shorts on without removing the condom, making his way to the bathroom so that he can make a total clean-up in one swoop. Alice is left to prepare herself for her morning yoga...

CHAPTER 4

FORGIVE ME, FATHER

MY NAME IS JACOB. Why, you might wonder, would you want to know? And why bother to even read any further? Well, my son, or daughter, I want to confide something in you. Something is hidden, something dark, but believe me, it is also exciting. Why do I want to tell you about it, you will ask yourself, since we are not even acquainted. Well, that, dear reader, is the point. What I have to tell you is not destined for the ears and eyes of a friend I have known my whole life. It is meant for someone like you, whom I have never met, whom I will never meet. I don't know your face, your name, and I want to leave it at that.

I am a priest. I have been for nearly 30 years, and I desire to remain in that position until the day I die. However, I need to get something off my chest, and would I tell anyone close to me about it, my life as a man of God would be over.

So here I am, sitting at my desk in my little chamber that is illuminated by the flickering light of a candle, writing these lines to you, my unknown friend.

Shall I continue now? Shall I tell you about my dark secret?

But where should I begin? Maybe with her auburn hair? With her enchanting smile? Or maybe with her sparkling eyes last night, after I had made love to her? Or should I tell you about her yelling my name in the dark and cold of the church when I thrust all my manhood into her?

I get aroused just thinking about how she bent over the altar, how I grabbed her sweet hips and pushed into her with all my might.

But, yes, let me start with the beginning when I finally gave in to the world of sweet seduction when she came to me to confess her sins and to receive proper punishment.

"Forgive me, Father, for I have sinned." I heard her sweet voice from the other side of the confessional box. I remained silent and let her explain.

"I touched myself this morning."

I closed my eyes and invariably pictured it. She had done this before, dozens and dozens of times, telling me all about it and getting me hot.

"Why did you do it?" My voice sounded strange and hoarse.

"I needed to satisfy my longing for you," she explained, her voice not more than a breath. She would always tell me I was the reason, she would always tell me she wanted me.

"So I had to do it," she added.

"What did you do?" My voice was a shivering mess.

"I unbuttoned my blouse and let my hand play with my breasts. My thighs opened and my other hand slid between them, under my skirt."

She gave a sensual sigh before she let me know the entire truth. "Like now."

Like now? My imagination went wild picturing this girl

in the adjacent booth with her legs spread and playing with her most sensitive part. To supplement this image I could hear the rustling of nylon and fabric.

Underneath my robe I was getting a huge erection, tempting me to do as she was doing. Her moaning was becoming more audible.

"What are you doing?" I intended this to be more as a rhetorical question than a real one but she decided to go with the latter.

"My hand is rubbing me...between my legs. It feels so good, Father." She moaned deeply, making me harder.

"I need something hard to penetrate me. Oh, Father."

I couldn't help it. My hand began to stroke the huge bump in my robe, knowing it was the hard thing she needed so badly.

"Oh." Just this little word revealed that she was about there – at her highest level of excitement.

She was ready to come. Her breath had gotten to an ecstatic rhythm of groaning.

"Are you..." I whispered hesitantly, not knowing how to handle the situation that was far too much, far too arousing for a priest like me.

"Yes," she exhaled like in a trance, interrupting my help-lessly stupid question. "Father." She almost yelled this word and I knew she had just climaxed.

For a moment there was silence. She tried to catch her breath and cleared her throat several times in embarrass-ment. I sat there with a big erection that just would not go away. All because of her.

In all these years nothing similar had happened. I had

always managed to keep my sexual desires under control. But now I was just not able to anymore. I had lost control.

"This is unacceptable," I muttered finally.

"Oh Father, forgive me," she pleaded remorsefully. "I don't know what came over me." "You'll be forgiven if you'll do what you're told."

"Yes." She was clearly embarrassed, ready to make up for her mistake.

"Go to the altar and wait there for me. You need some serious punishment."

I heard her leave the booth and was drunk with arousal, unable to think one clear thought. But I knew no one would be in the church since it was already nighttime.

When I stepped out of the confessional box I got mad with longing. There she was. A young, beautiful girl in a short skirt, all embarrassed and at the same time I could see her want me. I could see it in her eyes. The way she looked at me was just too intense, too erotic, she would never be able to hide her desire.

"Bend over," I ordered strictly.

She did, revealing the embroidery of her thigh-highs, and showing me she didn't wear any panties.

As a priest, I should be immune to those things but this girl made me forget any promise or vow I had ever given to God. In this situation, all I felt was the pounding, pulsating, fiery desire, manifested as that huge, extremely hard erection in my pants. It needed to be satisfied and satisfied it was going to be. I reached for the zipper underneath my robe to free my hardness in anticipation, not taking my eyes off that young, firm flesh that was being presented to me so willfully.

Before I even realized what I was doing my hand

slapped those cheeks, turning them into light red. She groaned every time my hand spanked her ass, and I no longer could take it. Another hit on her behind and my erection got so hard it was on the verge of being painful. Carefully I put my hand around it and guided it between her thighs. We both moaned as it touched her soft, gentle region. Now it was too late to turn back, I had to finish this, I needed to feel her. Slowly I began to rub my hardness between her legs, applying soft pressure. It felt so good, and when the tip finally reached its real destination, I held my breath, closed my eyes, and slowly, inch by inch, pushed into her.

At that very moment, I couldn't believe that I had stayed away from a feeling so incredible. I completely filled her, and when I started to move in her she willingly opened her legs for me, allowing me to thrust deeper, intensifying this feeling. Here, I lost the last bit of control I had left. Like a madman I shoved it in her, powerfully thrusting it in and out, always with the same fast rhythm, in and out.

"Father," she moaned in ecstasy. "It feels so good to have you in me." I gave a deep groan.

"It feels so good to put it in you," I responded breathlessly and did her even harder. The muscles in her pelvis got tense in the rhythm of my movements, additionally massaging my stiffness. I was unable to hold it any longer.

"I'm going to come right now, right in you," I panted heavily, feeling the force of an incredible climax building up within me. Me not having had sex in 30 years, you can probably guess what it felt like.

I grabbed her hips and lifted them up so I could thrust in as deep as possible, and all the sexual tension collected for 30 long years was being released in an immense explosion inside her.

. . .

It took me several minutes to calm down and recover from this unbelievable orgasm, but when I did, I made sure that little girl had her fun, too. And I assure you, she had. Me too. Several times more.

CHAPTER 5

SHE'S MINE

SHE LIKED THE UNEXPECTED, and when she came over, I didn't even hug her, didn't even kiss her. I certainly didn't expect that.

"Is something wrong?" Those puppy eyes again. I pulled her in through the door and slammed it behind her. Apparently, today was high heels day, which pronounced her thick and bi-table legs. A sight that would surely never get old for me. A skirt and a thong decorated those legs, making my dick stand at attention, almost as though it wanted to see just how fucking hot she looked. As I slammed the door, the look in her eyes caught me by surprise. I could see she didn't know what to think. She didn't need to think, however, all she would need to do this day is spread that thick, tight ass of hers. She didn't need to think, because I knew what she *would* think when this was over. And like always, I knew it would be hard for her to go back to her boring husband again. A fact that always gave me a certain kind of pleasure, a reason to smile.

.   .   .

"Did your husband not fuck you again?" I asked and grabbed her by the hips, pulled her close to me, and felt her excited breath upon my lips. I knew she felt it, a bulge in my pants pressing on her hip. Her breath quickened when she felt I was already hard for her. She nodded to my question. Those damn puppy eyes again. When a woman as hot as her shows up at your doorstep, you see, you have to wonder what kind of a man doesn't fuck a woman like that. It can only be a married man. A man who is fucking someone else. The scumbag was fucking someone else, and she knew it. Because of this, she needed me almost as much as I needed her. But I still didn't kiss her. Instead, I turned her and slammed her on the wall, grabbed her so hard between the legs she yelped as I lifted her. Grabbing her ass with my other hand, I squeezed it, and then set her down. I knew her getting a taste of my strength always gets her pussy dripping. I turned her around, got on my knees, slapped her ass, and bit the fabric separating me from her flesh. Those two meat chunks of hers stared at me, barely contained by her tight outfit. The girth of her ass made my mouth water. But unlike her attire holding in that juicy thing of hers, I couldn't hold myself in; I pulled down her skirt in one, swift motion and jammed my face between her legs. The wetness of her surprised me every time. The taste of her made my tongue move by itself. She jumped and moaned as I shook her ass, licked her fast, licked her slow, up, down, sideways, but never went in to her, not yet. She quickly had enough, her pussy dripping all over my face. She wanted more than my tongue, turned around, grabbed my hands, and tried to lead me to bed.

.   .   .

"We'll have none of that," I murmured. I locked her hands behind her, pressed myself on her ass and grabbed her nipple, pinched it, pulled it. I dry humped her. My other hand slipped to her neck and I squeezed until she turned red. She moaned as I let go of her and led her to the bedroom. I threw her on the soft mattress, her hair spilling behind her as she fell. The bed embraced her, and soon after so did I.

I wanted to look at her face as I placed my dick inside her, so I turned her on her back. We both wanted to feel each other. I wanted to feel myself inside her, just as much as I knew she wanted my cock. All of it was evident in her movements. The way she quickly undressed me, pants first, the way she pulled away from her shirt and licked my stomach, the way her tits bounced as she unclasped her bra. The glistening wetness of her pussy waited for me as she spread her legs wide. You know the type of pussy that just begs to be fucked? The type of pussy that makes you stop for a while and you just stare at it? She had that type of pussy. Better, in fact. But I couldn't wait and stare, I had done enough staring. It never ceased to surprise me just how good her pussy felt. It was like a fine wine. It was a taste to be savored. So the first time I always did it slowly. I watched as my cock spread those lips of hers and grabbed her hands. I pinned her down as I entered her fully and then slammed myself inside her. Her moan was delicious, like something out of a dream.

A moan as though she never had cock before. Her skin was soft beneath me, the feel of her pussy even softer. My hand again slipped around her neck. Her mouth waited for me, open as though expecting another cock to fill her. My fingers would do. I ran them across her full and wet lips first, all the while fucking her, her tits bouncing. I then ran my two fingers across her tongue, when the bitch bit me. I laughed and she smiled. We had those moments too when things went from "I am fucking you because I need you," to "I am fucking you because it's the most fun I can ever have." Her reward for that little bite of hers was me ramming her even harder, deeper.

All the way in, all the way out. I loved the way it looked when I did it, and she loved the way it felt when I didn't stop doing it. She didn't need to say it for me to know who she belonged to, but I knew she would. She spread her legs as much as she could and I pinned her down again as she began to cum. I could feel her pulsing around my cock. I grabbed her neck when I knew she wanted it the most, squeezed when I began to feel her thighs shaking, then planted a gentle kiss on her lips and heard her whisper what I wanted to hear, "I'm yours."

ABOUT THE AUTHOR

Chara Gladey is an emerging erotica author of many erotica kinks and sub-genres. Be sure to check out other books and leave a review if this story got you hot!

Visit my blog at Chara Gladey's Blog

Join my newsletter for the exclusive Chara Gladey's Newsletter

Sign up for Free Stories from Xplicit Press AuthorsCandra Aubrey's Blog

Xplicit Press Author Updates

Like Xplicit Press on Facebook

Follow Xplicit Press on Twitter

Readers: I want to expand a few of the stories to see where the characters can be explored further. If there are any of the stories that you would like to read more about again, I'd love to hear from you!

Keep In Touch
Chara Gladey
info@charagladey.com